ASHES FOR GOLD

A Tale from Mexico

Retold by Katherine Maitland
Illustrated by Elise Mills

Folklore Consultant: Bette Bosma

MONDO Publishing
980 Avenue of the Americas
New York, NY 10018
Visit our web site at http://www.mondopub.com

Printed in Canada

01 02 03 9 8 7 6 5 4

Photograph Credits Aurelio Flores/The Nelson A. Rockefeller Collection/The San An-
tonio Museum of Art: p. 17; Miriam Katin: p. 18; Joe Viesti/Viesti Associates: pp. 19, 21
top; Don Klumpp/The Image Bank: p. 20; M. B. Duda/Photo Researchers: p. 21 bottom.

Library of Congress Cataloging-in-Publication Data

Maitland, Katherine.
    Ashes for gold : a tale from Mexico / retold by Katherine Maitland ; illustrated by
Elise Mills.
        p.   cm.
    Summary: Tricked by a clever acquaintance, a poor Mexican still manages to turn
ashes into gold.
    ISBN 1-879531-14-3 : $21.95. — ISBN 1-879531-43-7 : $9.95. —
ISBN 1-879531-22-4 : $4.95
    [1. Folklore—Mexico.] I. Mills, Elise, ill. II. Title. III. Series.
PZ8.1.M286As   1994
398.21—dc20
[E]
                                                                    94-14349
                                                                        CIP
                                                                         AC

My favorite memories as a child are of listening to the Mexican folktales, or *cuentos*, told by my parents, relatives, and their friends. Some of these delightful tales were about the silly and foolish things that can happen to people. *Ashes for Gold* reminds me of these stories. It is a wonderful, humorous tale I know you will enjoy reading again and again.

JoAnn Canales

Once, there were two men. Pancho was poor and not very smart. Tomaso was clever.

"What is this?" Pancho asked.

"I sold ashes for money," said Tomaso. "See?"

But Tomaso was playing a trick.
He had sold flour, not ashes.

"Pancho, you should sell ashes, too."

Pancho ran off to gather ashes
from his fireplace.

It was a long walk into town. "Ashes for sale!" cried Pancho. People stared at him. "Ashes for sale! Sir, 1,000 pesos."

"Are you crazy?" said the man.

Pancho walked on. "Ashes for sale! Sir, 500 pesos."

"Are you crazy?" said the man. No one wanted to buy his ashes.

Pancho walked and walked. Finally, he came to the town square.

"Sir, I will sell you this bag of ashes for one peso!"

"One peso!" the man cried. "Your ashes are worth nothing. This fool's mask is what you get!"

"Ha-ha!" laughed the
people. "Look at the fool!"

Poor Pancho! Tomaso had played
a trick on him!

Cold and hungry, Pancho headed home. In the distance, he saw a campfire. Were these bandidos?

Pancho was afraid, but he was too tired to care.

The bandidos welcomed him.

Later, Pancho woke up, shivering. He pulled out the mask, and covered his face to keep it warm.

One of the bandidos woke up and saw the horrible face.

"Aieee!" he screamed. "Run for your lives!"

"Aieee! Aieee!" they cried.

Pancho woke up. Frightened, he ran after the bandidos.

"Wait for me!" he yelled. But it was too late. The bandidos had disappeared into the night.

"My mask!" thought Pancho. "My mask must have scared the bandidos!"

Slowly, Pancho walked back to the campfire. He saw a bag the bandidos had left.

"What is in the bag?" he thought. "Gold!" He saw two more bags.

"Gold! Gold!" Pancho danced up and down. "I am rich!"

Pancho hurried home.

Close to his hut, he met Tomaso.

"Ashes?" asked Tomaso.

"I sold the ashes," said Pancho.

Tomaso could not believe his eyes. "Ashes for gold?"

Now Pancho was a rich man. Never again was he hungry or cold.

And what do you think Tomaso did?

ike all people, Mexicans love to laugh at silly stories like *Ashes for Gold.* Such noodlehead tales are told for fun and to teach people to laugh at themselves when they are tricked or make mistakes.

Traditional Mexican clay model like characters in the story.

Silly Willy   **Jumoke**   **Big Anthony**   **Iktomi**

Noddlehead tales are told around the world. In the United States, people tell about the adventures of Silly Willy. In Africa, stories are told about a foolish boy named Jumoke who tricks a trickster, Anansi the Spider. In Italy, people tell about Big Anthony, who makes everyone laugh without ever knowing why. And the Plains Indians tell many tales about a silly man named Iktomi.

In *Ashes for Gold*, the artist uses the bright colors and patterns of Mexico. The characters wear colorful clothes like Mexicans wore long ago. The colors of the design around the pages match the colors in the pictures. The bright patterns were also very popular, and they are still used on clothes worn for traditional celebrations today.

Woman and man dancing at a celebration.

exico is a beautiful country. It has tall mountains and leafy trees in some parts and deserts with prickly cactuses in others. People make the country even more beautiful by putting baskets and pots of flowers everywhere.

Mexico City, the capital of Mexico, has the largest population in the world. It is a very modern city, but the colors and patterns of old Mexico can be seen all around. Even skyscrapers are sometimes decorated

Cactus plants in the desert.

Adobe buildings with red tile roofs.

with paintings called murals that show how Mexicans lived long ago.

Many people today live in mountain villages. Their homes often have orange tile roofs and are made of special clay bricks called adobe *(uh-doe-be)*. At busy outdoor markets, women and men sell the brightly colored toys, treat-filled piñatas, clay figures, and wood carvings they have made.

Piñatas shaped like animals.